Pink Ponies COOKBOOK

Barbara Beery

Photography by Zac Williams

GIBBS SMITH
TO ENRICH AND INSPIRE HUMANKIND

Salt Lake City | Charleston | Santa Fe | Santa Barbara

First Edition
13 12 11 10 09   5 4 3 2 1

Published by
Gibbs Smith
P.O. Box 667
Layton, Utah 84041

1-800.835.4993 orders
www.gibbs-smith.com

Designed and produced by Sheryl Dickert Smith
Printed and bound in China
Gibbs Smith books are printed on either recycled, 100% post-consumer waste, FSC-certified papers or on paper produced
from a 100% certified sustainable forest/controlled wood source.

Library of Congress Cataloging-in-Publication Data

Beery, Barbara, 1954-
  Pink Ponies cookbook / Barbara Beery ; photography by Zac Williams. — 1st ed.
    p. cm.
  ISBN-13: 978-1-4236-0510-2
  ISBN-10: 1-4236-0510-1
  1. Desserts—Juvenile literature. 2. Pastry—Juvenile literature. 3. Children's parties—Juvenile literature. I. Title.
TX773.B4174 2009
641.8'6—dc22
                                        2008048511

Contents

Sweet Treats

Pony's Favorite Apples ✳ 4
Strawberry Sweetie Pies ✳ 7
Pastel Pony Treat ✳ 8
Fairy Dust Lollipops ✳ 10
Marshmallow Cloud Fluff ✳ 13
Dreamy Pudding Pops ✳ 14
Ponytail Dippers ✳ 17
Jump-the-Fence Fruit Stack ✳ 19
Ponytail Pretzels ✳ 20

Savory Bites

Dainty Sandwich Dippers ✳ 22
Little Ponytail Puffs ✳ 24
Blossom Nachos ✳ 27
Pegasus Butterfly Biscuits ✳ 28
Sunny Meadow Sandwiches ✳ 31
Horseshoe Pasta ✳ 32
Little Filly Haystacks ✳ 35

Cookies and Cakes

Pony Pops Cupcakes ✳ 36
Pink Pony Cookies ✳ 38
Horsin' Around Cupcakes ✳ 40
Pony Party Ice Cream Cones ✳ 43
Catch-a-Star Cookies ✳ 44
Winner's Circle Donuts ✳ 47
Pink Berry Oat Bars ✳ 48
Carousel Cake ✳ 50

Dazzling Drinks

Prancing Pony Lemonade ✳ 52
Unicorn Punch ✳ 55
Morning Glory Milk Shake ✳ 56
Pony Park Teacups ✳ 58
Sunbeam Smoothie ✳ 61
Bluegrass Punch ✳ 62

Pony's Favorite Apples

Ingredients

8 wooden Popsicle sticks

8 Granny Smith apples, stems removed

1 (½ pound) package white candy coating

Pink sprinkles, nuts, and small pink and white candies

Let's start dipping!

Line a cookie sheet with foil and lightly spray with nonstick cooking spray.

Push a Popsicle stick down into the core of each apple. Put the apples in the refrigerator on prepared cookie sheet while making the candy coating.

Melt candy coating according to package directions. Let cool for 5 minutes.

Remove apples from refrigerator and dip each apple into coating, covering the apple at least three-fourths of the way up. Allow excess coating to drip back into the bowl or pan.

Roll apples in sprinkles, nuts, or small candies while the coating is still soft. Place decorated apples on cookie sheet and return to refrigerator for 30 minutes or until ready to serve. Apples may be refrigerated up to one day.

Crisp and sweet!

Strawberry Sweetie Pies

Makes 6 pies

Ingredients

1 small package instant white chocolate pudding

Milk

1 cup milk chocolate chips

6 strawberries

Assorted sprinkles

1 (6-count) package mini graham cracker pie crusts

Let's start mixing!

Line a cookie sheet with foil and set aside.

Make pudding with milk according to package directions. Cover and set in refrigerator until ready to use.

Melt chocolate chips in microwave according to package directions. Remove melted chocolate from microwave and carefully dip each strawberry into chocolate, then roll in sprinkles. Place strawberries on prepared cookie sheet and place in freezer for 10 minutes.

Divide pudding equally among graham cracker shells. Remove strawberries from freezer and place one strawberry on top of each mini pie. Chill pies in refrigerator until ready to serve.

You're a sweetie pie!

Pastel Pony Treat

Ingredients

1 pint vanilla frozen yogurt

1 pint strawberry sorbet

1 pint lime sherbet

1 to 1½ cups Marshmallow Cloud Fluff (page 13)

1 bottle purchased chocolate syrup

1 small bottle maraschino cherries with stems, drained

Assorted sprinkles

Let's start scooping!

In small glass bowls, place one scoop each of vanilla frozen yogurt, strawberry sorbet, and lime sherbet. Top with Marshmallow Cloud Fluff, drizzle with chocolate syrup, and top each with a cherry and sprinkles.

It's magical!

Fairy Dust Lollipops

Makes 12 lollipops

Ingredients

36 Jolly Rancher candies

12 lollipop sticks

Let's start melting!

Preheat oven to 300 degrees F. Line two cookie sheets with foil and spray lightly with nonstick cooking spray; set aside.

Place same-colored candies in a ziplock plastic bag and securely shut. Place in a second ziplock plastic bag and securely shut. With a rubber mallet or rolling pin, hit the candies and crush into small pieces. Or place the plastic bag on floor and "stomp" on the candies to crush!

Place approximately 3 crushed Jolly Ranchers very closely together in a circle with the pieces of candy touching on prepared cookie sheets. Leave 3 to 4 inches between each bunch of candy pieces. Make 12 bunches.

Bake for 5 to 6 minutes until the candy has melted. Watch closely and carefully remove from oven as soon as candy is melted. Insert lollipop sticks into each melted design. Allow candy to cool completely, about 30 minutes.

Remove lollipops from cookie sheets, cover ends with plastic wrap, and tie each with a ribbon.

A fairy-tale treat!

Marshmallow Cloud Fluff

Makes 3 cups

Ingredients

3 egg whites

2 cups light corn syrup

½ teaspoon salt

2 cups powdered sugar

1 tablespoon vanilla

Pink paste food coloring

Let's start mixing!

In a large bowl, combine egg whites, corn syrup, and salt. Beat with a mixer on high speed for 10 minutes or until thick.

Add powdered sugar, beating on low speed until blended. Beat in vanilla and food coloring.

Store covered in the refrigerator for up to two days. Use on cupcakes, cookies, and ice cream!

Float away on this sweet cloud!

Dreamy Pudding Pops

Makes 8 pops

Ingredients

- 4 cups vanilla or cherry yogurt
- 1 tablespoon honey
- 1 teaspoon vanilla
- 1 cup raspberries or sliced strawberries
- ¼ cup pink sprinkles
- 8 Popsicle sticks

Let's start mixing!

In a medium mixing bowl, combine yogurt, honey, and vanilla. Mix well with a whisk until smooth and creamy. Carefully fold in fruit and sprinkles.

Spoon into Popsicle molds, filling ½ inch from the top of each mold. Insert Popsicle sticks. Freeze for 4 hours or until ready to serve.

Dreamy and creamy!

Ponytail Dippers

Ingredients

1 package (3 ounces) cream cheese, softened

⅓ cup creamy peanut butter

¼ cup purchased chocolate syrup

½ teaspoon vanilla

2 tablespoons milk

Let's start dipping!

In a large mixing bowl, combine cream cheese and peanut butter. Beat with a mixer on medium until smooth and creamy.

Gradually beat in chocolate syrup, vanilla, and milk until well blended. Serve as a dipping sauce for pretzels, marshmallows, or fresh fruit such as banana slices, strawberries, grapes, and apple slices.

Dip in and enjoy!

Jump-the-Fence Fruit Stack

Makes 6-8 servings

Ingredients

1 cup fresh peaches, peeled and thinly sliced

1 cup fresh blueberries

1 cup fresh strawberries, thinly sliced

1 cup green grapes, halved

Let's start stacking!

Chill fruit in refrigerator. Layer the peaches, blueberries, strawberries, and grapes onto small serving plates. Serve immediately.

You'll jump for this treat!

Ponytail Pretzels

Ingredients

Flour for dusting

1 package (12 count) frozen roll dough, thawed

2 tablespoons water

1 tablespoon kosher salt

1 can purchased vanilla frosting

Assorted food coloring

Assorted colored sprinkles and decorating sugars

Let's start rolling!

Preheat oven to 425 degrees F.

Line a cookie sheet with foil and spray lightly with nonstick cooking spray; set aside.

Dust your work area with 2 tablespoons of flour. Take a roll and knead it. Then roll it into a snake shape. Repeat for remaining rolls. Place each rolled piece of dough onto prepared pan, leaving 1½ inches between each. To form a ponytail, twist up the bottom end of each piece of dough to create a curvy ponytail shape.

With a pastry brush, dampen the surface of each ponytail with a small amount of water. Sprinkle lightly with salt. Bake for 10 to 15 minutes or until lightly golden brown.

While pretzels are baking, divide frosting between several small bowls and color each with a different food coloring.

Remove baked pretzels from oven and cool on pan 5 minutes before removing to a cooling rack to cool completely.

Drizzle each with assorted colored frostings and decorate with sprinkles.

Ponytails with a twist!

Dainty Sandwich Dippers

Makes 6 dippers

Ingredients

1 teaspoon Dijon mustard

4 slices hearty white bread, crusts removed

4 squares thinly sliced Swiss or Gruyère cheese

4 pieces thinly sliced deli ham or turkey

½ cup + 2 tablespoons red raspberry seedless jam

2 eggs

2 tablespoons milk

¼ teaspoon salt

1 tablespoon butter

¼ cup powdered sugar for garnish

Let's start cooking!

Spread the mustard over 2 slices of bread. Top each with 1 slice of cheese, then 2 slices of ham or turkey, and then 1 more piece of cheese. Spread 2 tablespoons of the jam on the other 2 slices of bread, then firmly press them, jam side down, onto the bread with cheese to create 2 sandwiches.

Generously spray a heavy skillet with nonstick cooking spray and place over medium heat. As the skillet heats, whisk the eggs, milk, and salt in a shallow bowl until foamy, like soapsuds.

Place the butter in the center of the heated pan. Holding the sandwich together firmly, briefly submerge one side into the egg batter and then coat the other side.

Place the sandwich in the pan and grill on the first side for about 3 minutes, until golden brown. Flip it over with a spatula and grill on the second side for another 2 to 3 minutes.

Remove pan from heat and transfer the sandwich from the pan to a plate. Repeat for the second sandwich.

Heat ½ cup raspberry jam in a microwave-safe dish for 15 to 20 seconds until it is smooth like a sauce. Remove from microwave and set aside.

Slice each sandwich into 3 small finger sandwiches, sprinkle with powdered sugar, and serve immediately with raspberry dipping sauce.

A sandwich treat that is fun to eat!

Little Ponytail Puffs

Makes 12 puffs

Ingredients for Puffs

1 package frozen puff pastry, thawed

12 small smoked sausages

Ingredients for Dipping Sauce

⅓ cup ketchup

3 tablespoons honey

3 tablespoons apple juice

1 tablespoon soy sauce

Let's start baking!

Cut 1 sheet puff pastry into 12 slices, about 1 inch wide each, and return the rest to the freezer.

Preheat oven to 375 degrees F. Line a cookie sheet with foil and spray with nonstick cooking spray; set aside.

Roll each cut pastry strip around a sausage. Place on prepared pan and bake for 10 to 15 minutes or until golden brown.

While the puffs are baking, prepare the dipping sauce by whisking together all ingredients in a small bowl.

Remove puffs from oven, cool 10 minutes on pan, and then place on a serving plate. Serve immediately with dipping sauce.

A puffed pastry delight!

Blossom Nachos

Ingredients

6 whole wheat or flour tortillas

12 presliced squares American cheese

1 small can refried black beans

6 green olives with pimientos, cut in half

Let's start baking!

Preheat oven to 350 degrees F.

Line a cookie sheet with foil and lightly spray with nonstick cooking spray; set aside.

Using a flower-shaped cookie cutter, cut 2 flowers from each tortilla. Place on prepared pan and spray top of each cutout lightly with nonstick cooking spray. Bake for 5 to 7 minutes. Carefully remove pan from oven and cool for 5 minutes.

Cut each slice of cheese into a flower shape with the cookie cutter; set aside.

Spread about ½ teaspoon refried black beans onto each baked tortilla. Top each one with a flower-shaped cheese slice, and place an olive in the center of each.

Return pan to oven and bake for 5 to 7 minutes or until cheese begins to melt. Carefully remove from oven and serve immediately.

Bloomin' good!

Pegasus Butterfly Biscuits

Makes 20 biscuits

Ingredients

1 can (10 count) refrigerated biscuits

1–2 tablespoons flour

½ cup chopped bell pepper pieces, assorted colors

40 small pretzel twists

40 small pretzel sticks

Let's start baking!

Preheat oven to 350 degrees F.

Line a cookie sheet with foil and lightly spray with nonstick cooking spray; set aside.

Lightly sprinkle each side of biscuits with flour to keep the dough from sticking to your hands. Divide each biscuit in half, and form each half into a 2-inch snake shape by rolling the dough between your hands. This will make the butterfly's body. Place each onto the prepared pan.

Decorate the dough with several different colors of chopped bell pepper by pressing them lightly into the dough.

Insert 1 pretzel twist into each side of dough for the butterfly's wings. Then insert 2 small pretzel sticks at the top of the dough for the butterfly's antennae.

Bake for 6 to 9 minutes until biscuits are very lightly browned. Carefully remove pan and cool on a wire rack for 5 minutes before removing biscuits from pan. Serve immediately.

Take a bite before they fly away!

Sunny Meadow Sandwiches

Ingredients

12 slices whole wheat or white bread

1 tablespoon melted butter

2 tablespoons mayonnaise combined with 1 teaspoon ketchup

6 slices bacon, cooked and broken into small pieces

6 cherry tomatoes, sliced in half

½ cup shredded iceberg lettuce

6 cherry tomatoes for garnish

6 cornichons or tiny gherkin pickles for garnish

Let's start toasting!

Preheat oven to 350 degrees F.

Line a sheet pan with foil and set aside.

Cut out each slice of bread with a 2-inch butterfly-, heart-, or flower-shaped cookie cutter. Place each cutout on prepared pan and lightly brush with melted butter. Bake for 5 to 7 minutes. Carefully remove from oven.

Spread 6 mini toast pieces with the mayonnaise mixture and then top with equal amounts of bacon crumbles, 2 slices of cherry tomato, and lettuce. Top with plain cutout toasts.

Skewer 1 cherry tomato and 1 pickle onto a brightly colored toothpick. Stick into the center of each sandwich and serve immediately.

A plate full of sunshine!

Horseshoe Pasta

Ingredients

1 can (14 ounces) chopped Italian plum tomatoes, undrained

¼ teaspoon red pepper flakes

½ teaspoon garlic powder

½ cup whipping cream

½ teaspoon salt

1 package (12 ounces) horseshoe-shaped pasta, cooked and drained

½ cup grated Parmesan cheese

1 tablespoon minced fresh parsley

Let's start saucing!

In a saucepan over medium heat, combine tomatoes with their juice, red pepper flakes, and garlic powder. Cook uncovered, stirring occasionally, about 5 to 7 minutes.

Add cream and salt and simmer until sauce begins to slightly thicken, about 10 to 15 minutes. Remove from heat and toss with cooked pasta.

Sprinkle with Parmesan cheese and parsley and serve immediately.

You'll feel lucky to eat this horseshoe treat!

Little Filly Haystacks

Ingredients for Salad

2 cups coarsely chopped cooked chicken

2 stalks celery, chopped

½ red bell pepper, seeded and chopped

2 tablespoons chopped green onion

1 apple, cored and chopped

1 cup sliced green grapes

1 cup sliced and chopped iceberg lettuce

Ingredients for Dressing

¼ cup mayonnaise

2 tablespoons plum or strawberry jam

2 teaspoons freshly squeezed lemon juice

Salt and pepper

Ingredients for Serving

6 iceberg lettuce leaf cups

1 can (5 ounces) chow mein noodles

Let's start mixing!

Combine all salad ingredients in a large bowl. Set in refrigerator while making the dressing.

Combine the mayonnaise, jam, and lemon juice in a small bowl. Add salt and pepper to taste.

Remove salad from refrigerator and toss with dressing. Divide equally among lettuce leaf cups, top with chow mein noodles, and serve immediately.

Full of crunch for a perfect lunch!

Pony Pops Cupcakes

Makes 24 cupcakes

Ingredients for Cupcakes

1 box devil's food cake mix

Milk

1 teaspoon vanilla

½ teaspoon coconut extract

Ingredients for Frosting

1 can purchased vanilla frosting

1 cup powdered sugar

Pink paste food coloring

Lollipops in assorted colors, shapes, and sizes

Assorted hard candies

Let's start baking!

Preheat oven to 350 degrees F.

Line 24 muffin cups with paper liners. Lightly spray inside of each paper liner with nonstick cooking spray; set aside.

Prepare and bake cupcakes according to package directions, substituting milk for water and adding vanilla and coconut extract. When cupcakes are baked, cool on a wire rack for at least 30 minutes before frosting.

Combine frosting, powdered sugar, and food coloring in a medium bowl. Mix well to blend all ingredients. Frost each cupcake, piling frosting high in the center.

Insert lollipops into each cupcake and garnish the top surface with assorted candies. Serve immediately. You can store undecorated cupcakes in an airtight container for up to one day and decorate just before serving.

Join us in lollipop land!

Pink Pony Cookies

Makes about 24 cookies

Ingredients for Cookies

1 cup butter, softened

1½ cups sugar

1 egg

2 teaspoons vanilla

¼ cup rainbow sprinkles

2 teaspoons baking powder

1 teaspoon salt

3 cups flour

Powdered sugar for dusting

Horse-shaped cookie cutter

Ingredients for Royal Icing

3 tablespoons meringue powder

2 cups powdered sugar

¼ cup + 2 tablespoons warm water

1 teaspoon vanilla

½ teaspoon almond extract

Paste food coloring

Silver dragées for decorating

Let's start rolling!

Preheat oven to 375 degrees F.

Line two cookie sheets with foil and spray lightly with nonstick cooking spray; set aside.

In a large bowl, cream butter and sugar with an electric mixer. Beat in egg and vanilla. Stir in sprinkles.

In a separate bowl, combine baking powder, salt, and flour and blend with a whisk. Add to butter mixture 1 cup at a time, beating well after each addition. Dough will be stiff.

Divide dough in half and roll out to ¼ inch thickness on a work area that has been sprinkled with powdered sugar. Cut out cookies with horse-shaped cookie cutter. Dip cookie cutter into powdered sugar occasionally to keep dough from sticking.

Place cookies on prepared pan and bake for 8 to 12 minutes or until cookies are barely browned.

Remove pan from oven and cool on a wire rack for 5 minutes before removing cookies from pan. Cool another 15 minutes before frosting.

To make Royal Icing, combine meringue powder,

powdered sugar, water, vanilla, and almond extract in a mixing bowl. Beat on high speed with an electric mixer for 3 to 5 minutes.

Divide among separate bowls and add food coloring as desired. Ice and decorate cookies.

Pretty little ponies!

Horsin' Around Cupcakes

Makes 12 cupcakes

Ingredients for Cupcakes

½ cup butter, softened

½ cup sugar

2 eggs

1½ cups self-rising flour

2 teaspoons vanilla

½ teaspoon strawberry extract

Ingredients for Frosting

1 can purchased vanilla frosting

Pastel mint candies for decorating

Let's get mixing!

Preheat oven to 350 degrees F.

Line a 12-cup muffin pan with paper liners and spray each liner with nonstick cooking spray. Place muffin pan on a cookie sheet and set aside.

Combine butter and sugar in a medium bowl and beat together with a hand mixer until light and creamy. Add eggs one at a time and whisk until eggs are blended into sugar and butter. Stir in flour. Add vanilla and strawberry extract and mix until batter is smooth and creamy.

Divide batter evenly among muffin cups. Bake cupcakes for 12 to 15 minutes or until lightly browned and puffy. Carefully remove pan from oven and cool on a wire rack 30 minutes before frosting cupcakes.

Frost each cupcake generously with frosting and decorate with pastel mint candies or other candies as desired.

No horsin' around, these cupcakes are great!

Pony Party Ice Cream Cones

Makes 20 cones

Ingredients

20 rainbow-colored flat-bottomed cones

1 box confetti cake mix

Milk

2 pints strawberry ice cream

Sliced strawberries

Let's start mixing!

Preheat oven to 350 degrees F.

Place two muffin pans on two cookie sheets. Place ice cream cones in muffin cups; set aside.

Make cake mix according to package directions substituting milk for water. Divide batter evenly among cones, filling to 2 inches below top edge. Bake 10 to 12 minutes or until cupcakes are puffed and lightly golden brown.

Carefully remove from oven and cool in muffin pans on a wire rack for at least 30 minutes.

When ready to serve, top each cupcake cone with a scoop of ice cream and garnish with a strawberry slice. Serve immediately.

Perfect for a party!

Catch-a-Star Cookies

Makes about 30 cookies

Ingredients for Cookies

½ cup butter

¾ cup sugar

1 egg

1 teaspoon vanilla

1½ cups flour

4 tablespoons cocoa

½ teaspoon baking powder

½ teaspoon baking soda

¼ teaspoon salt

Powdered sugar for dusting

Ingredients for Icing

2 cups powdered sugar

1 teaspoon vanilla

1–2 tablespoons whipping cream

Pink and blue paste food coloring

Assorted candy decorations

Let's start rolling!

In large mixing bowl, cream butter and sugar together with a mixer. Add egg and vanilla and beat until light and fluffy.

In another bowl, combine flour, cocoa, baking powder, baking soda, and salt and whisk to blend ingredients. Slowly add dry mixture to creamed mixture, blending well. Flatten dough into a disc, cover, and chill in the refrigerator for 2 to 3 hours.

Preheat oven to 325 degrees F.

Line two cookie sheets with foil and lightly spray with nonstick cooking spray; set aside.

Divide dough into three sections, working with one portion at a time. Place on a work area that has been dusted with powdered sugar and roll to ¼ inch thickness.

Cut into star shapes with cookie cutters and place on prepared pans. Continue rolling out and cutting shapes until all the dough is used.

Bake cookies 8 to 10 minutes or until very slightly puffed. Carefully remove from oven and cool on pan on a wire rack for 10 minutes. Remove cookies from pan to frost and decorate.

To make icing, blend powdered sugar with vanilla and 1 tablespoon whipping cream. Stir until smooth, adding more whipping cream if necessary. Divide icing among 3 small bowls. Leave one white, add pink food coloring to one, and blue food coloring to another.

Catch some fun!

Ice cookies and decorate with candies. Store covered for up to 3 days.

45

Winner's Circle Donuts

Makes 8 donuts

Ingredients for Donuts

1 can (8 count) large size
   refrigerated biscuits

3 tablespoons butter,
   melted

Ingredients for Glaze

1 cup powdered sugar

2–3 tablespoons milk

1 teaspoon vanilla

Pink paste food coloring

⅓ cup sprinkles

Let's start baking!

Preheat oven to 375 degrees F.

Line a cookie sheet with foil and lightly spray with nonstick cooking spray; set aside.

Press each of the 8 biscuits into a 2½-inch round. With a 1-inch round biscuit cutter, cut a hole in the center of each biscuit or cut out the dough with a donut cutter. Dip all sides of donuts into the melted butter and place 1 inch apart on prepared pan.

Bake 12 to 14 minutes or until golden brown. Carefully remove from oven and cool for 5 minutes on pan.

To make glaze, combine all ingredients except sprinkles in a small bowl. Whisk by hand until combined.

Dip one side of each donut into the glaze and then decorate with sprinkles. Serve immediately.

Delightful dipped donuts!

Pink Berry Oat Bars

Makes 16 bars

Ingredients

½ cup butter, melted

½ cup sugar

½ cup brown sugar

1 egg

1 teaspoon vanilla

¼ teaspoon baking powder

¼ teaspoon baking soda

¼ teaspoon salt

½ teaspoon cinnamon

1 cup flour

¾ cup dried cranberries
or cherries

¾ cup rolled oats

1 decorator tube purchased
frosting

Let's start mixing!

Preheat oven to 350 degrees F.

Line an 8 x 8-inch baking pan with foil extending 2 inches past the edges of the pan on two sides. Lightly spray the foil with nonstick cooking spray and set aside.

Place melted butter, sugars, egg, and vanilla into a large bowl. Stir to blend until smooth.

In a small bowl, whisk together baking powder, baking soda, salt, cinnamon, and flour. Slowly add to butter mixture and stir until well blended. Stir in dried cranberries or cherries and oats. This dough will be stiff.

Spread dough evenly into prepared baking pan and bake for 25 to 30 minutes. Carefully remove pan from oven and cool on a wire rack for 15 minutes.

Remove from pan by holding both extended ends of foil and pulling up and out. Cut into bars and leave plain or decorate with frosting. Store in an airtight container for up to three days.

Pony's favorite oats!

Carousel Cake

Makes 12 servings

Ingredients for Cake

½ cup butter, softened

1 cup sugar

2 eggs

2 teaspoons vanilla

Pink gel food coloring

½ cup milk

¼ teaspoon salt

2 teaspoons baking powder

1½ cups flour

Ingredients for Frosting

¼ cup butter, softened

4 cups powdered sugar

2 tablespoons milk (plus more if frosting is too stiff)

1 teaspoon vanilla

Pink paste food coloring

Pink Pony Cookies (page 38) for decorating

Pastel mint candies, sprinkles, and candy stick for decorating

Let's start baking!

Preheat oven to 350 degrees F.

Spray one 8-inch round cake pan and one 6-inch round cake pan generously with nonstick cooking spray and then line with circles of waxed paper or parchment paper; set aside.

In a bowl, cream together butter and sugar with an electric mixer. Beat in eggs, one at a time. Stir in vanilla.

Stir a small amount of pink food coloring into the milk and set aside.

In another bowl, combine salt, baking powder, and flour. Add to the batter alternately with colored milk. Beat until smooth and creamy, about 1 minute. Divide batter between pans, putting more in the bigger pan, and bake 30 to 35 minutes. The smaller cake may be done a few minutes before the larger cake. Cakes should be golden brown.

Cool cake in pans 10 to 15 minutes, then carefully remove by placing a plate or rack over each pan and inverting the cake onto it. When cakes are cool, center the smaller cake on top of the bigger one. Let sit another 10 to 15 minutes before frosting.

To make frosting, beat butter in a large bowl with an electric mixer. Slowly add powdered sugar, ½ cup at a time, alternately with milk. Add vanilla. Stir in a tiny bit of pink food coloring. Add extra milk, 1 tablespoon at a time, if needed.

Decorate with Pink Pony Cookies, candies, sprinkles, and a candy stick with a candy on top.

A magical carousel ride!

Prancing Pony Lemonade

Ingredients

4   mason jars (1 pint each)
    with lids

4   lemons

8   tablespoons sugar

4   cups water

Ice

4   strawberries

Let's start shaking!

In each mason jar, combine juice of 1 lemon,
2 tablespoons sugar, and 1 cup water.

Put on lid tightly and shake well to blend ingredients. Remove lid, add ice, put lid back on,
and shake again.

To serve, drink straight from the jar or pour
each drink into a glass and garnish with a
strawberry.

Shake things up with
this sweet drink!

Unicorn Punch

Ingredients

1 bottle (64 ounces) cran-apple juice, chilled

1 bottle (2 liters) lemon-lime soda, chilled

1 pint vanilla ice cream, softened

1 jar (8 ounces) maraschino cherries with stems

Let's start scooping!

Combine cran-apple juice and lemon-lime soda in a large punch bowl. Stir to blend.

Using an ice cream scoop, place scoops of vanilla ice cream on top of punch.

Put cherries on top of ice cream and serve drink in glass punch cups.

A magical punch!

Morning Glory Milk Shake

Makes 2 servings

Ingredients

1 cup low-fat milk

½ cup unsweetened frozen strawberries

½ ripe banana

2 tablespoons powdered chocolate drink mix

1 teaspoon vanilla

2 teaspoons sugar (optional)

Edible fresh flowers for garnish

Let's start blending!

In a blender, combine milk, strawberries, banana, chocolate drink mix, vanilla, and sugar if using. Blend until smooth.

Serve with edible fresh flowers.

It's flowery fun!

Pony Park Teacups

Ingredients

½ gallon water

6 to 8 bags decaffeinated tea

Juice of 3 oranges

Juice of 6 lemons

⅓ cup honey

10 to 12 cinnamon sticks

Let's start brewing!

In a large pot over medium heat, bring water to a slow boil.

Carefully pour water over tea bags in a large heat-safe container. After 5 minutes, remove bags and discard.

Add orange juice, lemon juice, and honey to the tea and stir to blend.

Pour into teacups and serve with a cinnamon "ponytail" swizzle stick.

Sweet tea for the little fillies!

Sunbeam Smoothie

Makes 2 servings

Ingredients

- 1 cup orange juice
- 2 to 3 cups vanilla frozen yogurt
- 1 teaspoon vanilla extract

Let's start blending!

Combine all ingredients in a blender and process until smooth and creamy.

Pour into glasses and serve with a fancy straw.

A sunny, sweet way to start your day!

Bluegrass Punch

Makes 12 servings

Ingredients

1 bottle (20 ounces) blue sports drink, chilled

1 liter sugar-free raspberry-flavored sparkling water, chilled

½ cup blueberries

½ cup raspberries

Ice

1 bunch fresh mint

Let's start stirring!

Combine sports drink and flavored sparkling water in a large punch bowl.

Add blueberries and raspberries and stir gently to blend.

Place 1 to 2 ice cubes in a tall fancy glass or punch cup and add punch. Garnish with a sprig of fresh mint.

A fruity blue punch that will serve a bunch!

Collect Them All!

www.gibbs-smith.com

www.kidscookingshop.com